THE
SCARY
STORIES
FOR SLEEP-OVERS
ALMANAC

Compiled by Michelle Ghaffari

Material written by Mary Batten, Alison Bell, Eric Elfman,
Phyllis Emert, Michelle Ghaffari, Q. L. Pearce,
Jill Smolinski, and Tina Vilicich-Solomon

Illustrations by Bryan Baugh

LOWELL HOUSE JUVENILE

LOS ANGELES

CONTEMPORARY BOOKS

CHICAGO

To Isabelle and Melanie, who always want to hear "more scary stuff"
—M. G.

Publisher: Jack Artenstein
Director of Publishing Services: Rena Copperman
Executive Managing Editor, Juvenile: Brenda Pope-Ostrow
Editor in Chief, Juvenile: Amy Downing
Typesetter: Bret Perry

Library of Congress Catalog Card Number: 97-73828

ISBN: 1-56565-829-9

Lowell House books can be purchased at special discounts
when ordered in bulk for premiums and special sales.
Contact Department TC at the following address:

Lowell House Juvenile
2020 Avenue of the Stars, Suite 300
Los Angeles, CA 90067

Manufactured in the United States of America

10 9 8 7 6 5 4 3 2 1

CONTENTS

DO YOU DARE TURN THE PAGE?

Who knows what evil lurks within these pages . . . everything you need to make the best scary sleep-over party ever!

Haunt your houseguests with fearsome facts and terrifying true tales about haunted habitations, eerie events, creepy creatures, and much more. In addition, you'll find lots of scary activities, repulsive recipes, ghastly games, and creepy crafts that will provide you and your guests with hours of unearthly fun.

Whether you're planning a party or just want to treat yourself and a friend or two to a night of horror, there's only one problem you may encounter: No one will want to go to sleep— you'll be having too much fun! (Or, you may be too terrified to close your eyes. . . .)

CHAPTER ONE

EERIE EVENTS

Throughout the ages, people have reported earthshaking encounters with the ghastly and bizarre. Many scientists and journalists take these terrifying tales seriously—so much so, in fact, that they dedicate their lives to discovering the truth behind the rumors. Some of the subjects you'll be treated to are aliens, human beings that burn in a mysterious flare of fire, ghostly presences that cause chaos for people, and much more.

People have been telling the tales you are about to read for a long time. So why not try them out at your next all-night bash? They are sure to make perfectly menacing storytelling material for your sleep-over!

ALIEN ABDUCTIONS

There may not be anything creepier than the feeling that someone unknown is watching your every move. Do you ever feel like some power is forcing you to do things that you just can't explain? It could be that alien beings are to blame! Here are some reportedly true tales about outer space that are sure to send your sleep-over party into orbit!

In the wee hours of the morning on August 12, 1983, Alfred Burtoo, a seventy-eight-year-old fisherman, was fishing by a canal in Aldershot, Hampshire, England. A bright light passed over his head, and soon after, two alien beings about 4 feet tall in green overalls walked toward him. They took him aboard a very large metallic spaceship. While examining him, the aliens asked Alfred how old he was. The aliens then informed him that he was too old for their purposes and allowed him to leave.

Alfred was freed without any side effects. Too bad that wasn't the case for Barney and Betty Hill! While driving home from a vacation in Canada on September 19, 1961, this couple from New Hampshire spotted a bright object in the sky. They stopped their car to take a closer look at it through binoculars. What they saw was a large object shaped like a saucer with brightly lit portholes. Through the portholes, they spotted several beings wearing caps and dark uniforms. The Hills took off quickly in their car.

Once they returned home, the Hills realized they were unable to account for two hours of their time. Barney started having nightmares about meeting a UFO. He also began having problems with ulcers and high blood pressure, so he sought medical advice. A psychiatrist hypnotized Barney to try to get more information from him. While under hypnosis, Barney recalled that he was taken aboard the spacecraft and subjected to a physical examination by large-eyed aliens. Betty reported a similar experience.

Her examination involved a needle that was inserted into her belly button. After being studied by the extraterrestrials, the couple were released.

Another alien report, this time from Brazil, occurred in the early 1970s. On the morning of October 28, 1973, a truck driver in Brazil stopped to change a flat tire. He was approached by three alien beings in silver spacesuits that abducted him while on a mission to study the human species. Like the Hills, the trucker was unable to recall what happened to him during a two-hour period of time.

MEN IN BLACK

In many cases after someone encounters a UFO, three men in black suits come to the person's home or office and issue a warning to stop telling stories about the experience. Traveling in a new black car, usually a Cadillac, the men have dark complexions, strange hair, and voices that sound like a flat monotone or a scratchy whine.

They threaten, badger, and try to convince people that they didn't see what they thought they did. One person who was researching UFOs was told by a Man in Black (MIB), "If you don't stop, we'll kill you." At least one death has been connected to MIB.

Who are the MIB? Are they government agents? Or are they aliens trying to keep their presence a secret? Some people believe that they are simply the fantasies of the individuals who report them, but these strange men have also been seen by several impartial witnesses.

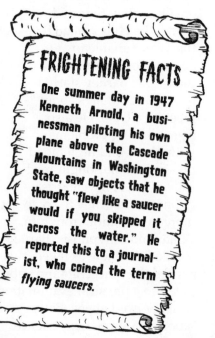

FRIGHTENING FACTS

One summer day in 1947 Kenneth Arnold, a businessman piloting his own plane above the Cascade Mountains in Washington State, saw objects that he thought "flew like a saucer would if you skipped it across the water." He reported this to a journalist, who coined the term flying saucers.

SPONTANEOUS HUMAN COMBUSTION

Ever wish you could make someone disappear in a burst of flame? Scary but true, there are many reported cases of spontaneous human combustion (SHC), the term used for instances where people seem to catch on fire from within their bodies. Often nothing more than ashes is left behind. Here are some fascinating cases of SHC:

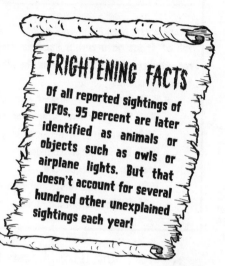

FRIGHTENING FACTS

Of all reported sightings of UFOs, 95 percent are later identified as animals or objects such as owls or airplane lights. But that doesn't account for several hundred other unexplained sightings each year!

- February 19, 1725—In Rheims, France, Nicole Millet was found dead with burns covering her body, while the armchair she was sitting in was not even singed.

- 1731—The Countess Cornelia di Bandi of Cesena, Italy, was found on the floor of her room. Her body was burned to ashes, except for half of her head, lying between her untouched legs.

- August 27, 1938—Phyllis Newcombe was dancing with her fiancé, Henry McAusland, at Shire Hall in Essex, England. Suddenly her body began to glow, and her dress flared up in flames. She burned to death almost immediately. Although the coroner tried to prove that a lit cigarette started the fire that killed her, it was

CREEPY CURIOSITY

Space aliens aren't the only beings that come from the skies. Since a rainfall of frogs occurred in Sardinia, Italy, in the year A.D. 200, people have reported creatures falling from the sky like rain. Here are some of the more famous incidents:

- 1578, Bergen, Germany—A shower of yellow mice
- 1877, Memphis, Tennessee—Thousands of snakes
- 1882, Iowa City, Iowa—Small blocks of ice containing tiny frogs
- 1896, Baton Rouge, Louisiana—Hundreds of dead birds, including wild ducks and woodpeckers
- 1959, Townsville, Australia—Numerous fish
- 1973, Brignoles, France—Tens of thousands of small toads

later found through tests that a cigarette could not have ignited the material of her dress.

- July 1, 1951—Only a few springs of her armchair, a badly charred skull, a slipper with a foot inside, and some bits of backbone remained of Mrs. Mary Reeser, a Florida woman who spontaneously ignited in flames. Upon opening Mrs. Reeser's door to deliver a telegram, the landlady of the building discovered her remains amid a huge blackened circle where Mrs. Reeser's armchair had been the night before.

- October 1980—A navy airwoman, Jeanna Winchester, was driving with her friend in Florida. All of a sudden Winchester lit up in flames and screamed, "Get me out of here!" They beat out the fire, but Winchester drove the car into a phone pole. Amazingly both survived, but 20 percent of Winchester's body was burned.

- October 3, 1987—An elderly Englishman sitting on a small sofa erupted in flames in front of his housekeeper.

Fire flew first from his nose and mouth, then his stomach. He died and the furniture was destroyed. Police were unable to find any evidence surrounding the fire.

GHOST GET-TOGETHERS

Telling ghost stories is the perfect activity for your scary sleepover. What follows are some favorite tales of terror, all based on true events.

THE GHOSTLY FLIGHT 401

On the evening of December 29, 1972, Eastern Flight 401 radioed the control tower at Miami that it was making its landing approach. The flight thus far had been perfect. Captain Bob Loft and Second Officer Don Repo were guiding the big plane's descent when the pilots discovered a problem with the landing gear warning light. It seemed to be a minor problem and just meant circling again to make a second landing approach. All fairly routine, or so the pilots believed.

As they worked on the landing gear, the pilots didn't realize that the plane had been steadily losing altitude. When they finally noticed how much altitude had been lost, it was too late to make a correction. The plane crashed into the dark Everglades, killing the crew and one hundred passengers.

When rescuers arrived, bodies were strewn everywhere. Captain Loft survived for about an hour after the crash but died in the cockpit. Don Repo was alive when rescuers pulled him from the wreckage, but he died in the hospital about thirty hours after the crash.

After the accident, to save money, Eastern Airlines officials decided to salvage parts from the wreckage and use them in other Eastern planes. It was then that many Eastern crew members began having strange experiences.

For almost two years pilots and flight attendants reported seeing the ghosts of Loft, Repo, and some unidentified flight attendants from Flight 401 on various Eastern flights. The ghosts were seen most often on planes containing parts from the plane that had crashed, but they were sighted on other planes as well.

Several times Captain Loft's ghost was seen sitting in a plane's first-class section. On one of these occasions a flight attendant asked Loft why his name was not on her passenger list. Her question was greeted with silence. The attendant went to her captain for advice. When the captain looked into the cabin, he instantly recognized Loft. At that moment the ghost disappeared.

Repo's ghost was seen even more often than Loft's. Crew members who saw Repo said that his ghost was especially concerned about safety. Sometimes Repo's ghost was seen in the cockpit checking instruments. Once Repo's ghost told a flight engineer that he had already made the pre-flight inspection. On other occasions he pointed out a problem in the plane's hydraulic system and warned an attendant about a fire on the plane.

Eastern employees who saw the ghosts were afraid to talk about them. Some of those who did were advised to see a psychiatrist.

Reports of the ghosts were so widespread that Eastern finally removed all the airplane parts taken from the ill-fated Flight 401. But they can't get rid of the memories, for no one who saw any of the ghostly crew will ever forget.

SPECTER SHIP

Bad luck hovered over the *Mary Celeste* long before she set sail. Built in 1861 in Nova Scotia, Canada, the ship was originally

CREEPY CURIOSITY

When journalist John G. Fuller heard about the ghost sightings, he knew there was a fascinating story to be told. He persuaded many Eastern employees who had seen the ghosts to tell him about their experiences. Their stories are reported in his book *The Ghost of Flight 401*. The book was published in 1976, and two years later it was made into a TV movie of the same name.

named the *Amazon*. Her first captain died two days after assuming command, and her initial journey came crashing to a halt when she plowed hull-first into a fishing boat off the eastern United States coast. While she was undergoing repairs, a fire broke out aboard ship, causing yet more damage.

In 1863, during a trip through the Straits of Dover in England, she hit another ship and sank it. In 1867, on another voyage, she ran aground on Cape Breton Island near Nova Scotia, requiring further repairs. The *Amazon* was rebuilt and sold to new owners, who renamed her the *Mary Celeste*. The ship was thoroughly refurbished and under the command of the able Captain Briggs when she left New York for Genoa, Italy, in late 1872.

On December 5, 1872, the sea was calm. But Captain Morehouse, the captain of the *Dei Gratia* and a good friend of Briggs, noticed the *Mary Celeste* bobbing aimlessly nearby in the ocean. He tried to contact the ship's captain. Having no luck, Morehouse sent crew members aboard the ship. What they found was baffling: The *Mary Celeste*'s decks were deserted. There was no sign of a struggle and all fourteen crew members and passengers were gone, along with the ship's small lifeboat—vanished without a trace.

Government officials, investigators, and journalists went wild with speculation. Did the ship's passengers fall into the sea while watching a swimming contest? Or did a drunk and

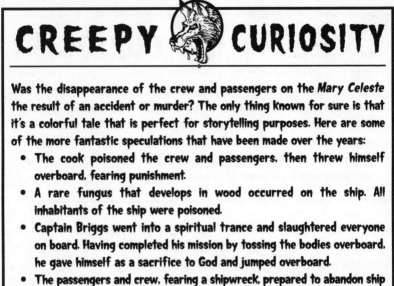

CREEPY CURIOSITY

Was the disappearance of the crew and passengers on the *Mary Celeste* the result of an accident or murder? The only thing known for sure is that it's a colorful tale that is perfect for storytelling purposes. Here are some of the more fantastic speculations that have been made over the years:

- The cook poisoned the crew and passengers, then threw himself overboard, fearing punishment.
- A rare fungus that develops in wood occurred on the ship. All inhabitants of the ship were poisoned.
- Captain Briggs went into a spiritual trance and slaughtered everyone on board. Having completed his mission by tossing the bodies overboard, he gave himself as a sacrifice to God and jumped overboard.
- The passengers and crew, fearing a shipwreck, prepared to abandon ship in a hurry. The lifeboat was placed in the water, but before the passengers could board, a gust of wind caused the lifeboat to drift away. The passengers were caught between the *Mary Celeste* and the lifeboat.

mutinous crew revolt, killing the captain and his family, then fleeing the scene in the ship's lifeboat?

In March 1923 a court determined that the fate of the *Mary Celeste* could not be reached with any certainty. The mystery remains unsolved.

POLTERGEISTS

Poltergeists are a perfect source for some of the scariest stories around. The word *poltergeist* is German and means "racketing spirit." These noisy, invisible beings can be quite destructive. Oftentimes the antics of a poltergeist start out being fairly childish and harmless but, if they continue, can become dangerous and ugly.

Poltergeist activity commonly takes place in households in which one family member is a boy or a girl between the ages of twelve and nineteen. The youngster, called the "poltergeist agent," is not physically responsible for causing the disturbance, although he or she may be in plain sight when an object is thrown from the other side of the room.

Poltergeists hurl objects, cause bad smells (usually sulfuric), slam doors, and break things. They most often inhabit one house, and some poltergeists even communicate with the people living in the house, usually by answering questions with knocks or raps. In any case, they always make their presence known.

Some families panic and abandon their homes. Others learn to live with their spirited guest or guests, and eventually come to accept them as part of the household. This is what happened with the family of Reverend Samuel Wesley in Epworth, England, in the early 1700s.

The Wesley family had ten children, so there was plenty of opportunity for the spirit to find a poltergeist agent. The spirit first "introduced" itself to the household in 1716 with a knock on the door and a deep, low groan. The maid and another servant opened the door and found no one behind it, so they decided someone was playing a prank and went back to their tea. But soon after, they heard another knock. This time it was loud enough to rattle the entire door. The servant went to the

kitchen and discovered a hand mill, used to grind grain, whirling around on its own. He later retreated to his bedroom for the night, only to be awakened by the sound of an invisible turkey gobbling next to his pillow. The servant then heard a man tripping over a pair of boots at the edge of the bed, but no one was in sight. The days that followed included much of the same otherworldly activity.

Sometimes the unseen poltergeist would knock on doors and windows. Other times it would sound its deep, inhuman moan. But at times it seemed to get bored of its usual games and would give the family a more frightening display. It showed itself as an animal on more than one occasion, appearing once as a bunny spinning around in the kitchen. Another time it wandered around the baby nursery in the form of a badger.

The Wesleys named their ghostly guest "Old Jeffrey" and tried to find humor in the poltergeist activity. Finally one morning, Old Jeffrey gave two knocks at the head of the stairs during the family's daily prayer ritual, then left for good.

LA LLORONA, THE WEEPING WOMAN OF MEXICO

Dressed in a long, flowing black or white dress, she is seen walking alongside rivers or on lonely roads in Mexico. Tears continually stream down her face. Who is she?

Many Mexicans and Mexican-Americans call her La Llorona, Spanish for "the weeper." They believe La Llorona is the ghost of an Indian princess, Doña Luis de Olveros, who lived in Mexico City around 1550. According to legend, the princess fell in love with a wealthy nobleman, Don Nuño de Montesclaros, and bore him two children. Although he promised to marry her, he married someone else instead. When Doña Luis found out, she was humiliated by his treachery and became hysterical with anger. With a dagger he had given her as a gift, she stabbed their children to death. Then she wandered the streets, crying desperately for her children. She was arrested, found guilty, and hanged. Her ghost is believed to be cursed to wander the earth forever, searching for the children she murdered.

Since the sixteenth century La Llorona has been seen throughout

Mexico and even in parts of the American Southwest. Many versions of the story and different descriptions of the ghost exist. Some say she has long black hair and long clawlike fingernails. In some accounts she is faceless; in others she has the face of a bat, a horse, or a vampire.

Like the ghosts in many other hauntings, La Llorona seems sentenced to eternal punishment. Those who have seen her ghost say that she weeps piteously. Sometimes she pauses to tell a willing listener about her horrible deed. Sometimes she hitches a ride, tells the driver her wretched story, and then disappears. Over and over she relives the chilling details of her children's murders.

Some people believe that anyone who sees La Llorona will die or have bad luck within a year. So hope that you never see La Llorona on a lonely Mexican road at night.

THE ROYAL GHOST

Mary Tudor (1516–1558) was the daughter of King Henry VIII and Catherine of Aragon. When she became queen of England in 1553, she rebuilt Sawston Hall, a residence near Cambridge, England, which had been burned down by her enemies. She supposedly slept in the grand Tapestry Bedroom in a four-poster bed.

Behind the bed is a passageway that leads to a secret hiding place where Roman Catholic priests hid during the religious wars of the sixteenth century. Since her death, the ghost of Mary has been seen coming through that passageway's door on many occasions.

There have been other unearthly activities, too.

17

Visitors sleeping in the room always report the same thing:
There are three knocks at the door, then the door opens and a
gray apparition slowly floats through the room and vanishes
into the tapestry on the wall. Other people have reported hearing the sounds of a virginal, Mary's favorite keyboard
instrument, coming from the drawing room. However, upon
investigating, the room has been found to be empty.

KINDRED SPIRITS

In some cases it's clear that ghosts have gotten a bad rap. In her
book *True Hauntings*, real-life ghostbuster Dr. Hazel M.
Denning tells the fascinating story of an English girl named
Rosemary Brown. In 1924, seven-year-old Rosemary awoke
one morning in her room to find an otherworldly visitor standing before her. The man, who had long hair and wore strange
old-fashioned clothing, reassured her immediately. He told her
that she had a special destiny and he would visit her again
when she was older. Then he vanished.

CREEPY CURIOSITY

Abraham Lincoln, the sixteenth president of the United States, may be the White House's most famous ghost.

The first person to see Lincoln's ghost in the White House was Grace Coolidge, wife of President Calvin Coolidge, who served from 1923 to 1929. More than 58 years after Lincoln's death, she reportedly saw his silhouette standing at a window in the Oval Office.

Although more than a century has passed since Lincoln was murdered, some people continue to report seeing his ghost or hearing strange sounds in the White House, especially in Lincoln's bedroom, now called the Lincoln Room.

Dutch Queen Wilhelmina once visited President Franklin D. Roosevelt and told him of hearing footsteps in the corridor outside the Lincoln Room, where she was spending the night. Upon hearing a knock at the door, she opened it and saw Lincoln standing before her. The queen fainted. Winston Churchill, the British Prime Minister, believed he saw Lincoln's ghost. Eleanor Roosevelt, the wife of President Roosevelt, often sensed Lincoln's presence, usually late at night when she was writing at her desk. President Harry Truman also believed he heard Lincoln walking about.

Rosemary forgot about the incident for several years until she saw a picture of the man in her high-school textbook. He was Franz Liszt (1811–1886), the famous Hungarian composer and pianist. More time passed until she was visited once again by the ghostly composer, who told her it was time to get down to business: the business of composing music.

While Rosemary had very little musical experience (she had taken only a few piano lessons in her life), Liszt supposedly introduced her to some other long-since-expired legendary composers with whom she would also work: Beethoven, Chopin, Bach, and Debussy, to name a few. Liszt gave her personal and professional advice, and told her that he and the other composers wanted their music to live on through people like her.

Her compositions, which she reported were actually written by famous dead musicians, gained attention in England's musical world. Many people in the field doubted her story. Finally a major music studio challenged her to write a new composition in front of some highly respected musicians. She was afraid, but Liszt persuaded her to rise to the challenge. She wrote a beautiful and complicated piece that was too difficult for her to play on the piano. She went on to become an internationally renowned composer. Her book, *Unfinished Symphonies: Voices from the Beyond,* contains more on her fascinating life.

PHANTOM FEMALE OF NOB HILL

One evening in 1876, the Sommerton family, the wealthy inhabitants of an extravagant mansion in the Nob Hill section of San Francisco, California, was torn apart forever. Just hours before eighteen-year-old Flora Sommerton was to attend her debutante ball—a party given to introduce wealthy young women into society—Flora fled from her home, never to see her parents again.

Apparently Flora's folks had decided on the man their daughter should wed—someone she did not care to marry. So

the girl fled the house, still dressed in the white gown she was to wear to the ball. After much searching, Flora's parents offered a huge reward for information on their daughter's whereabouts, but it was to no avail. They finally accepted their doctors' theory that the girl had lost her mind and would probably never be found.

In fact, Flora was rebelling against her parents' wishes. She had been too afraid to stand up to them, so she ran away instead. After many years, Flora died destitute and ill. Rumor has it that when her body was found in a poorhouse in Butte, Montana, in 1926, she was still dressed in the white dress. But Flora's spirit lives on. Many people have reported that Flora's ghost still walks the streets of her old neighborhood in San Francisco, dressed in the white gown she wore on the night of her debutante ball.

BAD LORD LONSDALE

Some ghosts are kindly, protective spirits; others are angry, returning to make life as miserable as possible for their living family members. Lord Lonsdale's ghost was one of the angriest ever known.

Even when he was alive in the late 1780s, Lord Lonsdale of Westmorland, England, was a mean man. He argued with his neighbors, beat the peasants who worked his land if they couldn't pay his high taxes of grain and livestock, and treated people so badly that they called him "Bad" Lord Lonsdale. No one ever knew him to do a kind deed in his life.

When Lord Lonsdale died, few people shed tears. In fact, everyone was relieved to have Lord Lonsdale's body in the ground, covered by 6 feet of dirt. Little did they know, they had not seen—or heard—the last of him.

Soon after Lord Lonsdale's burial, the relatives who continued living in his home, Lowther Hall, reported a great commotion on the upper floors. Night after night they heard the lord's bellowing voice, shouting angrily as he had done so many times in life. Other nights loud crashes echoed down the halls as if someone were throwing furniture or smashing chairs on the floor. Heavy footsteps and stomping were everyday occurrences.

The terrified relatives would huddle together in one of the rooms on the ground floor while the ghost went on its nightly rampage. "Sir, please leave us alone," they would plead. "We never harmed you in life. Leave us be."

When the house grew quiet again, they would tiptoe cautiously into the hallway. Sometimes the ghost would appear at the top of the great staircase and glower menacingly at those cringing below. There was no peace in Lowther Hall.

Nor was there much peace outside the house. Some nights neighbors said they saw Bad Lord Lonsdale's specter driving a ghostly black coach and whipping the phantom horses into a panic. When they saw the coach, people feared for their lives and tried to get their carriages off the road.

Sometimes terrified neighbors lost control and drove into a ditch.

For years Bad Lord Lonsdale's ghost terrorized people throughout Westmorland. Finally a neighbor who was wise in the art of quieting angry spirits used his skills against the ghost. No one knows exactly what he did, but whatever his secret, Lowther Hall and the countryside of Westmorland became peaceful once more. By the end of the nineteenth century, the ghost of Bad Lord Lonsdale was seen no more.

CHAPTER TWO

DICTIONARY OF THE VERY SCARY

Get ready—even your bravest buddies will feel chills running up and down their spines! This mini-dictionary features frightening creatures that have been the subject of scary stories around the world.

ADACHIGAHARA

The Adachigahara, a horrifying Japanese monster, is supposedly a female cannibalistic spirit. This terrible monster is often shown with a large knife, preparing to kill a youngster for her meal.

BASILISK

The horrid basilisk takes its name from the ancient Greek word for "king"—*basileus*—and is sometimes called the "king of the lizards." It is said to have been created when the egg of an unborn rooster was mistakenly hatched under a toad or a serpent. This creature has the wings

of a chicken, a rooster's head, and a dragon's tail.

The basilisk has also been called a cockatrice, perhaps because of its parentage. Whatever its name, this legendary monster is deadly. Some species have fiery breath that can burn up anything in their path. Others are able to turn unlucky people to stone merely by looking at them.

If you happen to meet a basilisk, you'd better hope there's a mirror handy. According to legend, your only chance of survival is to show the monster its own reflection, so that it will be turned into stone instead of you!

CAT

Cats have served as both accomplices and companions to witches and warlocks throughout history. Cats—along with ferrets, rabbits, owls, crows, toads, and other small animals—were believed to have magical powers. Oftentimes, especially during the British witch-hunts of the seventeenth century, owning a tabby meant possible trouble for people. Because of its association with black magic, a pet cat was often considered evidence during witchcraft trials. In fact, sometimes a cat owner already suspected of being a witch was found guilty because of his or her purring partner.

CREATURE FEATURE

One of the most famous of all serial slayers, Jack the Ripper made sure that no woman felt safe on the streets of London in the late 1880s. He stalked his victims, all prostitutes, then slashed their throats and mutilated their bodies, removing body parts to keep as souvenirs. Jack the Ripper's identity remains a mystery to this day.

DRAGON

This mythical winged beast is featured in the folklore of peoples across the globe. In these tales, the dragon spits fire and venom, has terrible jaws, and often possesses a tail topped with stingers. The typical dragon of medieval legend is a huge creature up to 50 feet long, with huge fangs to snap its victims in half and fiery breath to cook up any potential meal.

Because of its long, snaky body, the dragon is often called a serpent. With scales the size of dinner plates, the dragon also has sharp spikes along its back. Awesome batlike wings enable it to fly down from its mountaintop cave to frighten nearby towns.

Although it's not very easy, there are ways to kill a dragon. According to legend, on rare occasions one could sneak up on a

dragon as it lay sleeping on its mountain of stolen treasure. Because the dragon's skin is so tough, most of the great folklore heroes who slayed a dragon did so by finding a soft spot in the beast's scaly armor and driving a sword through it.

FRANKENSTEIN'S MONSTER

Frankenstein's monster is one of the most famous horror-story characters of all time. In 1818, Mary Shelley published her masterpiece *Frankenstein*, about a mad scientist, Dr. Victor Frankenstein, who was obsessed with giving life to the dead.

The scientist conducted his horrible experiments for nearly two years before he successfully brought his creature to life. Standing 8 feet tall, with yellow skin covering its gigantic frame, the monster had black hair, watery eyes, a shriveled complexion, and black lips.

Terrified by the monster he had created, Dr. Frankenstein ran from his laboratory, letting his horrible creation escape. The monster later confronted the doctor and begged him to create a companion for it. When Dr. Frankenstein refused, the monster swore to get even.

Soon Dr. Frankenstein's closest friends were murdered. After his wife was strangled by the monster, the

CREEPY CURIOSITY

Monstrum, the Latin word for "monster," originally stood for any freakishly deformed being—animal, plant, or human. Before the mid-eighteenth century, many people believed that such deformities were caused by evil spirits, and that these monsters were sent from the gods as a warning that disaster was about to strike.

Here is a list of some famous monsters found in Greek mythology:

Hydra—a many-headed water serpent that was killed by Hercules, a Greek hero

Sphinx—a winged monster with a woman's head and a lion's body

Chimera—a grotesque fire-breathing creature usually described as having a lion's head, a goat's body, and a serpent's tail

Minotaur—a giant cannibal man with the head of a bull

scientist became determined to kill the product he had worked so hard to create. The chase led him all over the world and ended among the ice floes of the North Pole. There Dr. Frankenstein died of exposure, and the monster disappeared into the frozen wasteland.

GHOST

A ghost is the restless soul of a dead person that refuses to leave the world of the living. Why would a ghost or spirit continue to roam about the everyday world? No one knows. Perhaps the person was cursed for the evil he or she did while alive. Or maybe the person died so traumatically that the spirit remained rooted to that one area. Often a ghost may simply want to correct a wrong done to it while it was alive.

FRIGHTENING FACTS

Ghosts have been called all sorts of names throughout history. Some of the most common are phantom, poltergeist, apparition, spirit, shade, specter, wraith, and haunting.

A ghost can make its presence known in many ways: some moan, weep, or sigh; others drag chains or blow out candles; some are revealed only as a cold, intangible presence. Animals are generally the first to sense a spirit.

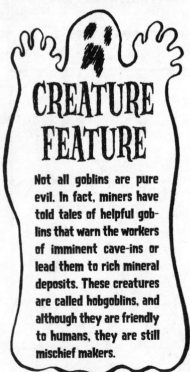

CREATURE FEATURE

Not all goblins are pure evil. In fact, miners have told tales of helpful goblins that warn the workers of imminent cave-ins or lead them to rich mineral deposits. These creatures are called hobgoblins, and although they are friendly to humans, they are still mischief makers.

GHOUL

A ghoul is a legendary graveyard creature that robs graves and feeds on dead bodies. In all likelihood once human, ghouls undergo an unexplained and horrible change after their death. Their human appearance becomes twisted, destroying their minds and robbing them of peaceful rest. Compelled to haunt graveyards, ghouls love to munch on young children or the fresh corpses of little ones. If none is available, ghouls will hunt down any living victims they can find.

GOBLIN

A goblin is a small, malicious, imaginary creature with a twisted body and deformed face that lives deep beneath the earth's surface. Many goblins can change their shape, appearing as animals such as toads or bats.

No matter what they look like, goblins are usually depicted as thieves or villains. Some legends say that goblins are companions to the dead. Others report that goblins like to tempt unknowing passersby into pits or traps to kill them just for fun.

Another way goblins catch victims is by enticing human beings to taste wonderful foods on display at a "goblin market." But beware! If a human actually tastes any of this marvelous fare, that person will die on the spot.

TALES OF TERROR

Each time you turn the page of one of these horrifying books, your palms will sweat, your spine will tingle, your heart will skip a beat or two. These titles tell some of the spookiest stories you'll ever hear. Pick out some favorite passages to read to your guests.

Frankenstein by Mary Shelley (1818)

The Raven and Other Poems by Edgar Allan Poe (1845)

The Strange Case of Dr. Jekyll and Mr. Hyde by Robert Louis Stevenson (1886)

The Picture of Dorian Gray by Oscar Wilde (1891)

Can Such Things Be? a collection of scary short stories by Ambrose Bierce (1893)

Dracula by Bram Stoker (1897)

The Phantom of the Opera by Gaston Leroux (1911)

The Haunting of Hill House by Shirley Jackson (1959)

KRAKEN

From the ninth to the eleventh century, the Viking warriors sailed the North Sea in their longboats. They thought the worst thing they had to face was the people of enemy lands. They had no idea that the North Sea is home to one of the scariest monsters of Scandinavian lore—the kraken.

Resembling a giant squid, the mythical kraken is reported to have ten or more snaky tentacles and is at least 50 feet long. When a kraken dives underwater, it creates a whirlpool that can suck a ship under. Many sailors tell stories of krakens that wrapped their many arms around unlucky vessels and dragged entire ships down to their underwater grave.

LOCH NESS MONSTER

Near the town of Inverness in the Scottish Highlands, a monster is said to swim deep in the Loch Ness waters (*loch* is the Scottish word for "lake"). Is it the last surviving plesiosaur (a marine reptile from the prehistoric Mesozoic era)? Or is it an evil, more magical monster? Nobody knows—the deep lake waters hide the answer.

Between the years 1639 to 1964, the Loch Ness monster has reportedly been sighted 360 times. In several reports the creature is described as approximately 30 feet long, with the snaky neck of a dinosaur and flippers on either side of its body. People have caught little more than glimpses of "Nessie," as it's fondly named by locals, so the creature remains a mystery.

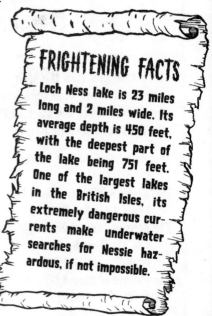

FRIGHTENING FACTS

Loch Ness lake is 23 miles long and 2 miles wide. Its average depth is 450 feet, with the deepest part of the lake being 751 feet. One of the largest lakes in the British Isles, its extremely dangerous currents make underwater searches for Nessie hazardous, if not impossible.

OGRE

In fairy tales, an ogre is one of the scariest types of giants. Unlike most giants, however, ogres are misshapen and not very smart. In fact, according to lore, most giants refuse to associate with their ogre cousins, whom they look upon with distaste.

The deformed ogre has a single activity that it thrives on—hunting human beings!

CREEPY CURIOSITY

Three types of mythical giants include Cyclopes (plural of Cyclops), trolls, and ogres. Although these creatures have distinct qualities, they do share some characteristics.

Size—Giants are huge! Some giants of legend grew to be 20 feet tall. In Scandinavian tales, trolls are huge, while stories from Denmark and Sweden tell of trolls the size of dwarfs.

Strength—Giants can throw large boulders the same way human beings can throw pebbles.

Appetite—Giants can really eat! One famous giant of medieval European lore, Gargantua, once ate five people in his salad.

Fun—Giants love riddles. One way to escape being a meal for a hungry giant is by challenging it to solve a riddle. (However, the giant must not be able to solve the riddle for the life to be spared!)

VAMPIRE

In Bram Stoker's *Dracula*, published in 1897, the most famous of all vampires, Count Dracula of Transylvania, stalked his victims at night, sucking blood from their throats.

More has been written about vampires than almost any other mythical creature of the night. They are said to be incredibly strong, and it's generally believed that they can change their shape at will, becoming a huge bat, a large wolf, or merely a vaporous cloud, in order to better hunt their victims or to escape their pursuers.

They are never seen when the sun is in the sky, even at dawn, since exposure to sunlight kills them immediately. No matter how far they roam at night, vampires always return to

CREEPY CURIOSITY

Count Dracula is one of the most famous fictional characters of our time. But the storybook count may have been based on a real-life blood drinker—Vlad V of Wallachia, a Romanian tyrant. This count earned the gruesome nickname of Vlad the Impaler because his favorite method of killing people was to impale them on posts while they were still alive. (His henchmen pushed a sharpened wooden pole upward through the victim's torso. This was done slowly to ensure that the victim suffered.) Other people believe the legend of Count Dracula was based on the notorious Hungarian countess, Countess Bathory, who was reported to have murdered hundreds of young girls and bathed in their blood!

their coffins, protected from the sun's rays.

What should you do if you encounter a vampire? There are many methods for repelling a vampire, according to legend. By wearing garlic, you may drive off a vampire temporarily. Also, a cross thrust into a vampire's face may cause it to back off, but it won't actually drive the creature away. A vampire can be totally destroyed only if it is exposed to sunlight, immersed in running water, or if a stake is driven through its heart. But watch

out—according to some legends, even these methods are not enough. The vampire's head must also be severed and its mouth stuffed with holy wafers.

WARLOCK

The warlock, or male witch, is a man who practices the secret art of magic. Also known as a magus, a sorcerer, or a wizard, the warlock generally uses his dark power to bring misery to all.

Merlin, perhaps the most famous warlock of all, was King Arthur's sorcerer. The son of a woman and a demon, Merlin used his strange and wonderful powers not for evil, but to serve the king.

A warlock can change his shape at will, becoming a stag, a greyhound, or even a tree. A warlock is also able to separate his soul from his body, which almost guarantees that he will never be killed.

WITCH

Like the warlock, the witch also possesses sinister magical powers. She guards her secrets closely, is usually depicted wearing a black cape and hat, and is often accompanied by her "familiar"—a common domestic pet like a cat or a dog that also has supernatural powers. A witch can tell the future and communicate with spirits.

CREEPY CURIOSITY

According to stories throughout the ages, witches and warlocks are disorganized, can't shed more than three tears, and hate salt. They have warts, dry skin, and dandruff. When they die, their bodies often melt, evaporate, or dissolve. The most evil ones come from the north and the east.

YETI

The Yeti—also known as the Abominable Snowman—is a mysterious creature that is said to dwell atop the icy peaks of the Himalayan Mountains of Tibet. It walks upright like a

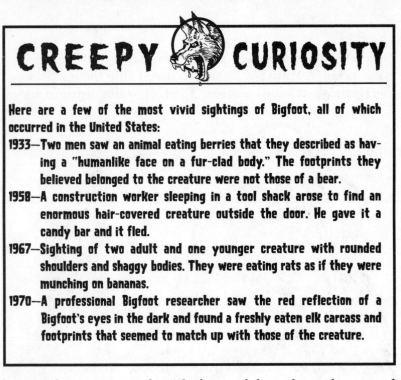

CREEPY CURIOSITY

Here are a few of the most vivid sightings of Bigfoot, all of which occurred in the United States:

1933—Two men saw an animal eating berries that they described as having a "humanlike face on a fur-clad body." The footprints they believed belonged to the creature were not those of a bear.

1958—A construction worker sleeping in a tool shack arose to find an enormous hair-covered creature outside the door. He gave it a candy bar and it fled.

1967—Sighting of two adult and one younger creature with rounded shoulders and shaggy bodies. They were eating rats as if they were munching on bananas.

1970—A professional Bigfoot researcher saw the red reflection of a Bigfoot's eyes in the dark and found a freshly eaten elk carcass and footprints that seemed to match up with those of the creature.

human but is covered with fur and has sharp fangs and claws like a bear. Its fur is all white, making the creature almost impossible to see in its snowy surroundings. While many scientists dismiss it as a myth, some believe it is a type of ape that really exists.

People all over the world tell stories of a very similar-looking creature found in their neck of the woods. Other names for the same type of creature include:

- Bigfoot or Sasquatch—United States (mainly in the Pacific Northwest) and Canada
- Skunk Ape—Florida
- Yeren (or Wildmen)—Asia
- Yowie—Australia
- Orang Pendek—Indonesia and Malaya

ZOMBIE

Deep in the hot and humid jungles of Haiti, the most feared monster is the zombie.

A zombie is a dead person that allegedly has been brought back to life by the evil magic of a voodoo witch doctor. This body lacks intelligence and a soul and will obey the commands of the witch doctor. People fear this monster for the harm it is capable of inflicting while serving a voodoo-practicing witch doctor.

One theory is that people become zombies when they have been given poison that sends them into a coma. Their loved ones are told that they have died, and they are buried. Shortly after the funeral service, the bodies are secretly dug up, and the people are revived. The witch doctor, or whoever is holding these poor people captive, continues to feed the victims a drug that keeps these zombies in a state of confusion.

FUN BUT FRIGHTENING FLICKS

Rent a couple of these, and you'll be set all night long for the perfect scary sleep-over! (Always get a parent's permission before renting any movies!)

Dracula (1931)
Frankenstein (1931)
King Kong (1933)
Invasion of the Body Snatchers (1956, 1978)
The Blob (1958)
Psycho (1960)

The Birds (1963)
The Night of the Living Dead (1968)
An American Werewolf in London (1981)
Poltergeist (1982)
Ghostbusters (1984)

CREEPY  CURIOSITY

Funerals around the world can be tremendously elaborate and expensive, or much more simple. And in some cases, the burial rituals are quite morbid.

- In Scythia: A king's funeral included the execution of his horses and slaves so that they could be buried with him.

- In Egypt: The Egyptians buried their rulers with wooden and clay models of their houses, boats, slaves, and animals.

- In the United States: Americans follow the customs of burial (inhumation) or cremation. American Plains Indians once buried their dead on platforms, sitting beside them for two days to keep the dead company and protect them against wild animals.

- In Scandinavia: At one time, Scandinavians buried their dead at sea, by laying the corpse on a funeral pyre on a ship, setting it ablaze, then sending it out to sea.

- In India: Anyone who buries the dead should be punished, according to the *Zend-Avesta*, an Indian holy book. Instead, the dead person is supposed to be placed in a tree or on a scaffold.

- Parts of Africa, New Guinea, and the Pacific Islands: In these places, cannibalism is thought to still be practiced, and it's not uncommon to eat the dead during a funeral feast. It is believed that one who eats an enemy or respected elder will receive the wisdom, strength, or courage of the dead.

PETRIFYING AND PECULIAR PLACES

*What makes one place scarier than another?
A cold, clammy breeze in a place with no
windows . . . a chilling voice with no
apparent source resonating in rooms . . .
a feeling that someone is watching you even
though you are alone. Take a look at ten of
history's most horrifying places and
spaces of torment. You may never want to visit
them, but you'll love telling your friends about
each one at your super-scary slumber party.*

TOP TEN PLACES NOT TO VISIT

1. BETHLEHEM HOSPITAL, LONDON, ENGLAND

In the mid-fifteenth century, Bethlehem (also called "Bedlam") Hospital, the oldest institution in England for the mentally ill, was thought to cure the insane. But perhaps the patients would have been better off left alone rather than suffer the evils performed at this place.

39

Authorities at the hospital invited people to come and have a look at the "loonies." And what a show they got! Patients were confined to damp, dark, straw-filled cells most of the time, and there were no wards for sick patients. The keepers at Bethlehem were masters of restraint—at least when it came to holding down the patients. Chains, belts, wrist locks, leg locks, belts, and gloves were all used. It was common to chain and whip "madmen" in asylums. One particularly violent patient, an American marine named James Norris, who was admitted on February 1, 1800, was able to remove the manacles from his hands and use them as a weapon. For the next nine years, he was confined in an iron harness, with a collar and chain that allowed him to stray no further than the side of his bed.

2. SALEM, MASSACHUSETTS

In 1692, a group of teenage girls claimed they had been bewitched by various members of the community. The girls exhibited bizarre behavior such as barking, screaming, and choking for no apparent reason. They accused many of the older, respected Salem women of witchcraft, claiming to have seen the women meeting with the devil. Thus began the famous Salem witchcraft trials.

The only evidence against the accused was what the magistrates called "spectral evidence," which basically meant anything the girls said was held as truth. The accused women were subjected to a body search for the devil's mark. Often a common birthmark or mole was considered proof of witchcraft.

If a woman was lucky enough to have a body free of blemishes, she was brought to court to confront the girls, who

CREEPY  CURIOSITY

Witches have been associated with broomsticks since the fifteenth century. Brooms have also been a symbol of female power. Sweeping with brooms was believed to drive away evil spirits. When they weren't at home, women in England left their brooms outside to safeguard the house. Gypsies and newly married couples in Wales completed the wedding ceremony by leaping over a broomstick when entering their new home.

screamed and convulsed in her presence. Supposedly touching a witch would make the girls powerless, so each hysterical teen was forced to touch the accused, and lo and behold, the girls suddenly calmed down and acted normally. The magistrates took this as additional spectral evidence.

Before the witchcraft scare ended, nineteen men and women had been hanged and numerous others were imprisoned. The young, persuasive girls held in their hands the power of life and death in Salem, until they accused the governor's wife of being a witch. The governor then ordered all those accused of being witches to be freed, and the trials ended.

3. STONEHENGE, WILTSHIRE, ENGLAND

Stonehenge was built on Salisbury Plain in Wiltshire, England, and dates back before written history. No one knows who built this famous circle of stone slabs, or why. A few researchers

think it was strictly an astronomical observatory. Others feel it may have been used to keep track of the seasons. Many people think Stonehenge was primarily a sacred place used by priests. Legend has it that the stones possess magical powers, and many visitors have reported witnessing strange lights and sounds near the stones.

4. BERMUDA TRIANGLE, ATLANTIC OCEAN

Also known as the Devil's Triangle, the Bermuda Triangle is an area in the Atlantic Ocean marked by Miami, Bermuda, and Puerto Rico at its corners. Over one hundred airplanes and ships have vanished within the Triangle. One minute the ship or plane is there, the next minute it's gone—the radar blips just disappear from the screen.

One of the survivors of a Bermuda Triangle close call was Captain Don Henry. While guiding his tugboat from Puerto Rico to the Florida coast on a bright, clear afternoon in 1966, Captain Henry heard his crew shouting. His compass began to spin wildly, the skies grew dark, and the boat's electricity failed, even though its generators seemed perfectly able. Water was coming at the boat from all directions, yet the surrounding sea appeared calm. As soon as they passed beyond the parameters of the Triangle, all systems returned to normal. A coincidence? Or were they some of the few lucky enough to survive the Triangle's mystery?

5. EL PANTEÓN CEMETERY, GUANAJUATO, MEXICO

Every year thousands of thrill seekers make their way through the catacombs, or underground passages, at El Panteón Cemetery in Guanajuato, Mexico. For a nominal fee they can view the more than one hundred mummies on display there—bodies that were originally buried in the cemetery directly above but were exhumed from their graves when families or

friends could not afford to pay for the grave maintenance. The ancient mummies of Guanajuato have been around since before the twentieth century. Because of the extremely dry Mexican climate and the high amount of salt in the soil, the bodies generally have not decomposed but have been preserved in all their other-worldly horror.

When descending the stairway to the catacombs, you come to a vaulted corridor where the mummies are on display. There you are free to examine their withered remains up close—if you have the stomach for it, since they are not wrapped in gauze like mummies in the movies. In the well-lighted corridor the mummies stand or sit in dreadful silence behind their individual glass coffins. Some of them reach out with open arms as if pleading. Others appear to be struggling, as if trying to break out of their confinement.

But it's the faces of the mummies that, once seen, will become imprinted in your mind forever. The awful, empty eye sockets seem to stare directly at you. The skeletal mouths hang open in silent but eternal screams, revealing long incisors that look more like fangs than human teeth. Some of the mummies wear shoes and have facial hair, with remnants of burial clothes draped over their parched and withering remains.

One thing is certain: No one—not even the most die-hard horror buff—can be completely prepared for what awaits visitors in the catacombs beneath El Panteón Cemetery.

6. DEVIL'S HOLE, NIAGARA GORGE, NEW YORK

The Devil's Hole cave extends approximately 20 feet deep into the rock, about 3 miles below Niagara Falls and high above the whirling waters of Devil's Hole Rapids in the Niagara Gorge. A large boulder called Ambush Rock stands in front of the cave opening and was once thought to have completely covered the entrance.

Stories about the cave originated hundreds of years ago when ancient Seneca Indians in the Niagara region believed the cave to be the home of the devil. They called it the "abode of the Evil Spirit" and avoided the area so as not to disturb the demon within.

Supposedly the stream that passes through the ravine near the cave once ran red with the blood of soldiers massacred by Indians in September of 1763. It is now called Bloody Run. For many years after the Devil's Hole Massacre, remnants of human bones, pieces of wagons, and parts of guns were found strewn among the rocks in the gorge below the cave.

Many accidents and tragedies are associated with this gloomy, dark cave. Are Indian legends true—is it the home of

CREEPY CURIOSITY

Below you'll find some of the strange but true occurrences at Devil's Cave.

June 28, 1854—A five-year-old girl falls 150 feet to her death near Devil's Hole.

September 6, 1901—President William McKinley rides the Great Gorge Railroad past Devil's Hole and hours later is hit by an assassin's bullet. He dies eight days later.

March 12, 1907—Just past Devil's Hole, a sheet of ice crushes a railroad conductor to death. He had stepped out of his train to throw a switch on the tracks.

July 1, 1917—A railroad car near Devil's Hole derails and plunges into the river below, killing fourteen passengers and injuring twenty-eight.

September 5, 1932—A fourteen-year-old boy falls to his death on the railroad tracks near Devil's Hole.

1935—The Great Gorge Railroad route, which passes Devil's Hole, is abandoned when a 5,000-ton avalanche uproots the tracks.

1982—Two young men were attacked and injured by unknown assailants. That same year a 15-foot boulder crashed down into the gorge, narrowly missing a twenty-five-year-old man.

1987—In separate incidents, two men were drowned in the river flowing below Devil's Hole.

an evil spirit or demon? Some say it's the winding pathways and rocky cliffs that make Devil's Hole such a danger zone. Others believe that those who mysteriously lost their footing or were involved in accidents near the cave may have been controlled by certain supernatural forces.

7. THE TOWER OF LONDON, LONDON, ENGLAND

Terrified screams, headless ghosts, phantom figures, disappearing apparitions, floating heads—it's all routine at the Tower of London, historically one of the bloodiest spots in the world.

Used for several hundred years as a prison, the tower is complete with a torture chamber and an execution site, and hundreds of people were hanged or beheaded there. Their ghosts still frighten visitors and haunt the Tower grounds today.

One of the most horrible executions that occurred in the Tower of London was that of Margaret, the Countess of Salisbury, in 1541. The seventy-year-old noblewoman, sentenced for treason, did not die with dignity. She was led screaming to the executioner's block, then she escaped from the guards and ran around like a crazed maniac. The guards had to drag her back to the block and force her to bend down. Ax in hand, the executioner missed not once but *four* times, before the fifth blow finally severed her head from her body. Countess Margaret's terrified screams are reportedly still heard near the site of her death on or near the anniversary of her execution.

Today the Tower of London is a museum.

8. ALCATRAZ, SAN FRANCISCO, CALIFORNIA

Walking down the now-vacant corridors of what was once the U.S. Penitentiary at Alcatraz, one finds the cell doors propped open, one after the other, displaying the empty, stark cubicles. A strange and eerie timelessness hovers in the air, as if the past were permanently imprisoned within the same walls where so many convicts were once locked behind bars.

While the halls have been empty for years, some security guards and tour guides have reported hearing odd sounds—screaming, whistling, even the sound of feet running along the corridors.

For nearly thirty years the U.S. Penitentiary at Alcatraz, part of the Golden Gate National Recreation Area and a popular tourist attraction, was a place of violence, brutality, and loneliness.

In 1933, the Department of Justice acquired the island of Alcatraz, and the following year, on July 1, it became a U.S. penitentiary. It was converted to a maximum-security prison due to a nationwide crime wave in the 1930s. Dangerous,

CREATURE FEATURE

The ghost most often seen by tourists and guards at the Tower of London is that of Anne Boleyn, the second wife of King Henry VIII. Anne was beheaded in 1536 after she was found guilty of being unfaithful to the king. The real reason for her execution was that she didn't bear Henry a son and heir to the throne. Divorce was not recognized by law at the time, and the king wanted to be free to take a new wife. Anne's ghost, with and without her head, has been seen alone or in a procession, usually close to the Bloody Tower (as it was called) where she spent her last days.

difficult, and desperate inmates were sent here to serve "hard time." Murderers, rapists, and gangsters, they included the likes of Al Capone and Machine Gun Kelly.

Completely surrounded by San Francisco Bay, Alcatraz, sometimes called "The Rock," was supposedly impossible to escape from. Conditions were bad at Alcatraz, but the worst were found in solitary confinement cells in Block D (nicknamed "holes" by the inmates). There many men became ill, went insane, or died. A prisoner was beaten and kept in complete darkness in a tiny cement cell with only a hole in the floor for a bathroom.

FRIGHTENING FACTS

The most famous escape from Alcatraz occurred on June 11, 1962, when Frank Lee Morris, and brothers Clarence and John Anglin, chipped out a tunnel through concrete and then used the prison ventilation system to escape from the cell house. They made their way to the water and were never heard from again. To this day it's uncertain whether the men drowned or actually escaped to the mainland.

Bread and water were fed to the prisoners twice a day, and every third day they were given a full meal.

9. AMITYVILLE HOUSE, LONG ISLAND, NEW YORK

For over two decades a house in Amityville, Long Island, has been hopping with supernatural activity. Doors open by themselves, people hear footsteps, and apparitions appear and disappear. But nothing has been as gruesome as what happened on the night of Friday, November 13, 1974.

Sometime around three A.M., Ronald DeFeo, Jr., shot and killed the other six members of the DeFeo family while they slept. When authorities arrested and questioned Ronald, he said repeatedly that something or someone else had taken over his body.

Hans Holzer, a world-famous parapsychologist and author, brought a psychic photographer and a reputable medium—Ethel Johnson Meyers—to the DeFeo house. While in a trance, she discovered that the house was built atop a sacred Indian burial ground. The Indian spirits were angry and out to seek revenge because someone had dug up a skeleton many years before.

Meyers told Holzer that people living in the house fought and never knew why. Supposedly they were possessed by an Indian whose presence she felt in the house. Apparently the spirits are alive and well, and the house has been sold many times over!

Many skeptics doubt any truth behind the supernatural occurrences in this house. Whether or not the Amityville home is truly haunted, *seven* movies have been made based on the horrors that allegedly took place there.

10. WINCHESTER MYSTERY HOUSE, SAN JOSE, CALIFORNIA

The Winchester Mystery House may be the most haunted house in the United States. In fact, its owner, Mrs. Sarah Winchester, renovated the home especially to please its ghosts.

Sarah was married to William Winchester, the son and heir to the Winchester rifle fortune. When William died in 1881, Sarah was grief-stricken and alone. Although William left Sarah $20 million, the fortune was little comfort in her grief. She told friends she had no reason to live.

Sarah believed that the dead communicate with the living through people known as mediums. One Boston medium had a message for her from William that said: "You will be haunted forever by the ghosts of those who were killed by Winchester rifles unless you do something to make up for their untimely deaths." According to the medium, Sarah needed to move West and buy a house for the ghosts to inhabit. Also, as long as Sarah continued to build onto her house, the ghosts would not harm her.

In 1884, Sarah moved to California and bought an eight-room house and 44 acres of land in San Jose, south of San Francisco. She hoped to build a house that ghosts would want to haunt, and for thirty-eight years she kept crews of workmen busy twenty-four hours a day, seven days a week, including holidays. As the years of construction continued, the house grew into a rambling mansion with miles of twisting corridors and secret passageways concealed in walls.

When eighty-three-year-old Sarah died of natural causes in 1922, she had spent most of her adult life trying to please ghosts. By then the mansion's four stories contained 160 rooms, 10,000 windows, and 2,000 doors.

All building stopped when Sarah died, leaving certain rooms in the mansion unfinished.

Today the grounds and a portion of the house are open to the public. Visitors to the house often report a variety of strange events there: windows suddenly blowing open on a calm, still day; sounds of an organ such as the one Sarah once played; lights mysteriously going on; doorknobs inexplicably turning on locked doors; and the apparition of an old woman. Many believe Sarah Winchester's spirit now haunts the mansion, joining the company of the ghosts she spent her life trying to please.

CREEPY CURIOSITY

The Amityville House certainly isn't the only family home better off avoided. This "home, sweet home" in Southern California offered its owners a lot more than they bargained for!

In 1856, San Diego businessman Thomas Whaley built a house on the property where a hanging scaffold had once stood. It was a fine home, and Thomas and his wife, Anna, gave many parties. But a few restless, noisy spirits also inhabited the house. One of the ghosts was "Yankee Jim" Robinson, who had been hanged for theft four years before on the spot where the Whaley house now stood.

In 1964, a televised séance was held in Whaley House by talk-show host Regis Philbin, who saw an image of a woman float from the study, through the music room, and into the parlor where he was sitting.

At least four ghosts are believed to dwell in the house now: Anna and Thomas Whaley, Yankee Jim, and a child known as the Washburn girl, who was a playmate of the Whaley children. Sometimes a phantom dog runs through the house, a baby cries, and a woman, believed to be Anna's spirit, sings. Cooking odors come from an empty kitchen, the odor of Thomas Whaley's favorite Havana cigars drifts from the main hall, and Anna's sweet-scented perfume is noticed all over the house.

CHAPTER FOUR

THE SCARIEST SLEEP-OVER EVER—YOURS!

You've read it all, from creepy creatures you wouldn't want to meet to haunted habitations you wouldn't dare to visit. Now's the time to put it all together and scare up a party that has everything, from devilish decorations to fiendishly fun food for those all-night creep-outs!

CHOOSING THE BEST FRIGHT NIGHT

You can make your sleep-over scary no matter what day of the week you have it. But if you pick your party night from these creepy days, chances are good your friends will be scared to death . . . and love it!

FRIDAY THE THIRTEENTH

Friday is thought by many to be the unluckiest day of the week, and 13 is considered in some cultures to be a very unlucky number (buildings in America are often built without a thirteenth floor). When the two are teamed up, watch out.

A FULL MOON

Just as people long ago believed that night was the evil opposite of day, they believed the moon to be the evil counterpart of the sun and feared it. Light from the full moon was thought to transform werewolves into their beastly form. It was also believed that if a moonbeam hit you while you slept, you could go insane.

53

HORRIFYING HOLIDAYS

January 6—Epiphany. Witches like to borrow brooms on this night, so be sure to hide yours! All through Europe it is believed that on this night the dead rise from their graves and walk the land.

March 22—The Feast of Cybele. An ancient Near Eastern festival during which a pine tree was cut and taken to the temple of the goddess Cybele. There it was wrapped in linen and mourned over like a corpse.

March 24—The Day of Blood. On the Day of Blood, which is the culmination of the Feast of Cybele, a high priest drew his own blood as an offering in tribute to Cybele.

April 24—St. Mark's Eve. Sit inside a church at midnight on St. Mark's Eve and prepare yourself. According to English lore, you may witness ghosts of all the townspeople who will die in the coming year enter the church.

April 30—Walpurgis Night. It's the Ball of the Year for witches, especially in Germany. Be sure to stick a thorn in your door on the night of April 30 so that witches won't be able to enter your house.

May 1—Beltane, or May Day. Human sacrifices took place during this festival of the Druids (priests of the Celts, an ancient people who lived in the British Isles thousands of years ago).

June 23—Midsummer's Eve. This night and the following day are probably the best times for practicing magic. It was—and still is in some parts of Europe—the occasion for huge fire festivals.

October 31—All Hallows' Eve (Halloween). Another great witches' sabbath and fire festival. It was believed that on this night and the following day, the Day of the Dead, the dead returned to earth. People used to leave food outside for them but would stay indoors themselves.

HALLOWEEN

Halloween was first celebrated as a Celtic festival honoring the dead. Between the seventh and eighth century A.D. the Catholics declared the first of November to be All Saints' Day, which became All Hallows' Day (hallow means "holy"). The day before, October 31, became All Hallows' Eve. By the sixteenth century the holiday was called Hallowe'en. So how did such a somber holiday turn into something as irreverent, spooky, and fun as Halloween?

FRIGHTENING FACTS

Midnight is commonly thought of as the time when witches meet to perform their magic. It is also said to be when the dead rise from their graves and when sorcerers' spells are most effective.

Many centuries ago, the Celts inhabited much of Europe. For them, the beginning of November marked the end of the year. Summer was over, the crops were already harvested, and the Celts dreaded the dark, cold winter that was about to begin. The first of November was celebrated as the Day of the Dead. Later Celts held a festival called Samhain, or "end of summer," to mark this event. People greatly feared the eve of Samhain, when the mortal and supernatural worlds met and the power of evil triumphed over good. Demons, witches, and other evil spirits ran amuck, and the souls of the dead returned to earth, sometimes to avenge wrongs done to them while they were alive.

Many current traditions stem from this time. Huge bonfires were lit to frighten off the ghosts, demons, and witches. Candy and other delectables were set out to make the evil spirits happy and keep them from doing harm. People wore costumes in order to ward off or fool demons.

PLANNING YOUR SINISTER SLEEP-OVER

Although the thought of conjuring up a visit from a bloodsucking vampire or a meat-eating zombie may not be your cup of tea, if you follow these tips, you'll plan a party so fun that it's sure to raise the dead!

First, before you do any planning, be sure to get permission from your mom or dad. (Otherwise, things are likely to get really hair-raising!)

Think about the best place for your party. Do you have a dark, dank basement or attic already decorated with real cobwebs? Why not pitch a tent in the backyard and tell ghost stories under the stars?

Next, make your guest list. A party can be just as scary with a group of friends or just one special friend or family member. Or make the party for yourself! It's easy to treat yourself to some heart-stopping terror with nothing more than a particularly petrifying book.

INHUMAN INVITATIONS

Ready to call your evil spirits together? Let guests know about your scary sleep-over with these terrifying tombstone invitations. Include all the devilish details, like the date, time, and location. Instead of R.I.P. (Rest in Peace), write R.T.P., which means Ready to Party!

What You'll Need

- gray origami paper
- black pen

Directions

1 Begin with paper cut in the shape of a square, at least 6". Fold the left and right sides about an inch in from the edges. Then fold the form in half, bringing the top to the bottom.

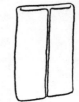

2 Fold the form in half once more, this time bringing the left side to meet the right. Then unfold your form to make a crease down the center. Fold again to bring each side to the middle crease, then unfold.

3 Make two more creases by folding and unfolding the top left and right points.

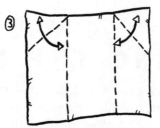

4 Now open the left side slightly. Push down on the left corner and tuck the fold inside. Repeat this step with the right corner.

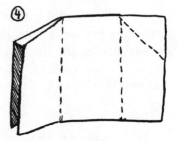

5 A black pen is all you need to mark this grave.
With big block letters, write R.T.P. Include the date, time, and location of your party, then sign it with a ghastly and goofy name like Frank N. Stein or Vanna Pire.

SETTING THE STAGE

What makes a scary movie or a haunted house at a carnival such a great adventure? Ghoulish sounds and ghastly visual effects that create a mood of terror. Try out some of these terrifying tips for deathly decor and sinister sounds. You'll turn your home into an absolutely abominable abode.

SINISTER SOUNDS

ADULT SUPERVISION REQUIRED

You can make a bevy of unbelievably sinister sounds just by using objects found in your house and some imagination.

What You'll Need

- several items for sound effects: soft-drink bottle, TV, TV remote control, lightweight poster board, rice, aluminum pan, cellophane paper, nails, tin can
- scary CDs and CD player; or scary cassettes and cassette player
- cassette recorder
- blank cassettes

Directions

1 Search your house for items that can be used as scary sound-effects props. With these, you'll imitate scary sounds. (Check the What You'll Need list for ideas.)

2 Get together one or several scary soundtrack CDs or cassettes, like those from *The Addams Family, Batman, The Frighteners,* and *Tales from the Crypt* (check your local library's supply of soundtracks, or ask your parents and other friends).

3 Line up your props on a tabletop near the TV and CD or cassette player.

4 Listen to the soundtrack and choose a few songs that sound eerie, sad, or spooky. Then think about how you can add some scary sound effects of your own. Here are some ideas:

- For ghostly moans, blow softly over the top of a soft-drink bottle.
- For alien voices, turn on your TV, then hold your finger down on the channel clicker. The snippets of sound from the changing channels sound like garbled space-creature speech.

- For monster footsteps, pound your palms, one by one, on a table or other hard surface.
- For terrifying thunder, rattle a sheet of lightweight poster board.
- For pounding rain, pour or sprinkle rice into an aluminum pan.
- For raging fires, crinkle cellophane paper.
- For rattling chains, shake a handful of nails in a tin can.
- For tortured screams . . . just scream! The shriller the better!

5 After you've practiced for a while, put a blank tape in the cassette recorder and put on your first scary song. (If your song is also on a cassette, you'll need two cassette players.) During the song, you can turn down the music and add your own scary sound effects that you think work well with the music. Then put the tape on as your friends come into your house, and watch how quickly everyone gets in the right mood for the party!

DEATHLY DECOR

Now that you know how to add sounds that will send chills up your friends' spines, you can hide some Hideous Hands throughout the house, make your own Ghastly Goblin Lanterns, or create a creepy atmosphere with lights. These creative design ideas will turn your humble home into a cemetery of celebration.

HIDEOUS HANDS

Stick these severed hands in the creepiest of places—a friend's sleeping bag, the bathtub, or hanging partially out of a drawer!

What You'll Need

- white or thin plastic surgical gloves (the kind doctors use—found at a pharmacy or drugstore)
- tissue paper
- blue, black, and red paints or markers
- strips of gauze bandage (¾" or 1" wide)
- white glue

Directions

1 Stuff gloves with tissue paper.

2 Color black or blue fingernails on the gloves with paints or markers.

3 Wrap gauze bandage strips around the entire glove, separating the fingers, until you reach the fingertips. Glue gauze down as you work.

4 Use red paint or marker at the wrist end of the hand to give it a severed look. (The stuffing may hang out a little. Just color it red to make it look like bloody insides!)

5 Hide your Hideous Hands throughout the house, and save some to sneak into your friends' sleeping bags before bedtime. Have one hand peeking out of a partially closed drawer. Try tying another to a doorknob.

GHASTLY GOBLIN LANTERNS

ADULT SUPERVISION REQUIRED

These creepy candleholders will send unbelievably spooky shadows straight up your walls.

What You'll Need

- several large green peppers
- cutting board
- sharp paring knife
- medium-sized spoon
- black marker
- several green or black birthday candles
- matches

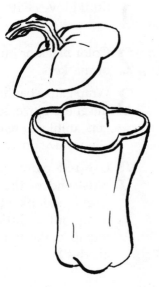

Directions

1 With a parent's help, place one green pepper on a cutting board and carefully cut off the top of the pepper around the stem. Make the hole only big enough for you to get a spoon into.

2 Use the spoon to scoop out the inside of the pepper. You may need to use the knife to get all the seeds out.

3 Choose one side of the pepper as your goblin face. With a black marker, draw a pair of eyes, a nose, and a mouth. The creepier the expression, the better! With the help of a parent, you are now ready to carve out the face. Move the knife carefully along the black lines you drew, cutting all the way through the skin of the pepper. Remove each pepper piece as you cut it out.

4 Now you need to cut a place to hold the candle. With your knife, make an indentation on the bottom of the inside of the pepper. This time, though, you don't want to cut through the pepper skin, so don't carve too deep.

5 Place a birthday candle in the bottom of the pepper. If the candle is too tall to fit inside the pepper, light the candle (with a parent's help) and let it burn down, then blow out the flame and put it inside. Carefully relight the candle.

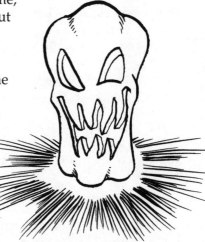

6 Repeat these instructions several times; after all, the more goblins, the more scares! Then dim the lights and tell ghost stories by the ghoulish light of your Ghastly Goblin Lanterns!

LIGHTS

By replacing regular lightbulbs with spooky colored ones, you'll create a whole new atmosphere in your house. Just consult a parent first and tell him or her what you are thinking of doing. Then visit your local grocery store or a nearby lamp store or hardware store. The colors that are easiest to find and that work the best are green, blue, and red. If you can't find colored bulbs, use felt-tip markers to color white ones. Try dark blue, purple, and orange for some really cadaverous colors.

REPULSIVE RECIPES

No party would be complete without some delicious snacks to munch on. But for your scary sleep-over, you'll want to dig up some gross goodies that will tempt friends with the most horrific bad taste! You can either make these snacks before your friends come over, or else have all the ingredients and cooking utensils handy so that you and your friends can stir up something especially sickening together. Be sure to go over the recipes you plan to make with an adult first—you'll probably need some help in the kitchen.

CRUNCHY BONES CANDY

ADULT SUPERVISION REQUIRED

Wrap this candy in aluminum foil or black tissue paper. Then watch with delight while your friends suspect that they're biting down on more than some delectable sweets—like bones, anyone?

Ingredients

- 1 tablespoon margarine or butter to grease pan
- 2 cups maple syrup
- 2 cups sugar
- 2 pounds semisweet chocolate chips
- 2 cups crunchy peanut butter
- ½ cup salted peanuts

- 10 cups Rice Krispies or raisin bran

Tools You'll Need

- 13" x 9" baking pan
- saucepan
- mixing spoon
- large mixing bowl
- knife

Directions

1 Grease baking pan and set aside. Place the maple syrup and sugar in a saucepan and, with an adult's help, bring the mixture to a boil, stirring continuously.

2 Remove from heat, add chocolate chips, and stir until the chips are almost melted but still have some lumps. Add peanut butter and peanuts and mix well.

3 Pour cereal into large mixing bowl. With an adult's help, pour the peanut butter and chocolate sauce over the cereal and stir until combined. Transfer the mixture to the greased baking pan and refrigerate for at least one hour. Cut into bone shapes.

Makes 50 ½" pieces

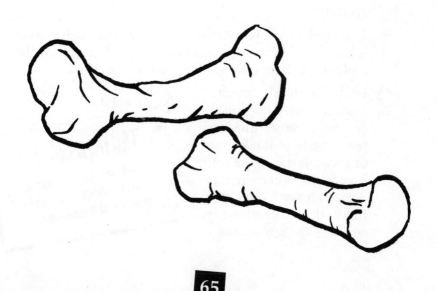

DRACULA'S
SECOND-FAVORITE DRINK

Most people know that vampires love to drink blood. Here's a special brew you can make that Dracula—and your friends—will slurp up by the glassful!

Ingredients

- white grape juice
- seedless green grapes
- 1 quart cranberry juice
- 1 quart lemonade or orange juice
- ½ cup raspberry sherbet

Tools You'll Need

- two ice cube trays
- black marker
- clear plastic glasses
- mixing spoon
- large pitcher
- spoons
- straws

Directions

1 To make Dracula Ice, fill ice cube tray so that each section is half full with white grape juice. Insert a grape into the center of each ice cube section. Freeze until solid.

2 Using a black marker, draw a spider, cockroach, or other creepy crawler on the outside of the bottom of each plastic glass. Your friends will feel more than a bit queasy when they think that something is crawling in their drinks.

TANTALIZING TIP

Float ice cube trays in warm water for easy removal of Dracula Ice.

3 About 10 minutes before serving, mix cranberry juice
   and lemonade or orange juice together in a large pitcher.
   Add sherbet and stir until it melts.

4 Add two pieces of Dracula Ice per glass. Fill each glass
   with juice mixture in pitcher. Serve with a spoon and
   a straw.

Serves 10 to 12 vampires

TASTY BIG TOES

ADULT SUPERVISION REQUIRED

Follow these directions to make delicious short breadsticks that look like toes!

Ingredients

- refrigerated breadstick dough
- olive oil
- Parmesan cheese
- black olives, pitted
- spaghetti sauce

Tools You'll Need

- knife
- cookie sheet
- pastry brush (or clean unused paintbrush)
- serving plate
- small bowl

Directions

1 Unroll precut breadsticks and cut each in half. Shape ends of breadsticks to resemble toes. Place on ungreased cookie sheet.

2 Brush breadstick toes with olive oil and sprinkle with Parmesan cheese. Slice black olives in half to stick on the ends of the toes for toenails.

3 With an adult's supervision, bake according to directions on breadstick package.

4 Serve on a platter with a small bowl of spaghetti sauce, for those who love dipping their toes in a little "toe jam"!

Makes 16 big toes

TERRIFYING TEETH

ADULT SUPERVISION REQUIRED

Feeling a little like a cannibal? These tasty treats really smile back at you when you're about to bite down on one!

Ingredients

- 3 apples
- 12 tablespoons peanut butter
- mini-marshmallows

Tools You'll Need

- sharp paring knife
- butter knife
- serving plate

Directions

1 With an adult's assistance, cut apples into eight slices each and remove core (leave skin intact).

2 Spread 1 tablespoon peanut butter on one side of each half of the apple wedges.

3 Press mini-marshmallows into the peanut butter on the outer side of each apple wedge to make teeth.

4 Put an apple wedge, peanut butter side down, on top of each apple slice with marshmallows, pressing together to form a mouth. Arrange mouths on a serving plate.

Makes 12 mouths

BLOODY NOSE SOUP

ADULT SUPERVISION REQUIRED

Keep a few extra tissues nearby for this delectable dessert.

Ingredients

- 1 20-ounce bag frozen raspberries, thawed
- 1¼ cups water
- 1 cup cran-raspberry juice
- ½ cup granulated sugar
- 1½ teaspoons ground cinnamon
- 3 whole cloves
- 1 tablespoon lemon juice
- ½ cup sour cream

Tools You'll Need

- blender
- large saucepan
- pot holders
- large strainer
- large heat-safe serving bowl
- wire whisk
- ladle
- 4 to 6 small serving bowls
- kitchen tablespoon

Directions

1 With an adult's help, pour raspberries and water into blender container, put lid on, and puree. Pour into a large saucepan.

2 Add in the cran-raspberry juice, sugar, cinnamon, and cloves. With an adult's help, bring mixture to a boil over medium heat. Use pot holders to remove from heat and pour through a strainer and into a heat-safe serving bowl. Allow to cool. Add lemon juice and whisk until completely blended. Place in

refrigerator until you're ready to serve.

3 Just before serving, ladle Bloody Nose Soup into bowls. Use a kitchen tablespoon to drop dollops of sour cream (cotton balls) onto center of each bowl of Bloody Nose Soup. Serve chilled.

Serves 4 to 6 nosy neighbors

PUTRID PRESENTATION

Squirt red frosting so that it appears to be dripping out of your nostrils. Then serve the soup like there's nothing wrong. When everyone lets you know your nose is bleeding, just wipe it off and eat it. Explain that it's sometimes hard to make the bleeding stop after you're finished filling the bowls.

GHASTLY GAMES

You've set the stage. Now it's time to play games and tell spooky stories that will keep you partying all night long!

TELL A TERROR-FILLED TALE

You've read about some of the most dangerous creatures, eerie events, and haunted habitations known to humans. Use this grisly info to create some of the scariest stories yet!

What You'll Need

- colored lightbulbs
- flashlight

Directions

1 Turn the room lights off and turn the colored lightbulbs on.

2 Gather your friends into a circle and tell them that each party guest will play a role in telling these tales. A flashlight will be passed to whoever is speaking.

3 Start the game by telling the beginning of a ghost story. If you like, use one of the two examples below to get you started:

"Deep in my heart, I knew that I was making a mistake. The afternoon was quickly turning to evening, and the sky began to turn dark. The wind was beginning to howl, and with it came dark clouds, threatening to storm. . . ."

—or—

"I was on my way home from school, and I found myself walking by the graveyard. The wind was whipping around me so hard, it pushed me into the cemetery. I soon found myself standing on a grave. Just as I turned to run away, something, or someone, grabbed me by the . . . "

4 Stop at the climax and pass the flashlight to the person on your left. He or she will fill in the next part of the story, stopping with another unfinished sentence. Continue going around the circle as long as everyone is having fun and adding to the story. The last person should create the ending—as sick and scary as the group can handle.

TANTALIZING TIP

If you record the story on a cassette recorder, you can play the story back to the group and decide whether the story is creepier or funnier the second time around.

THE SPOOKIEST STORYTELLING EVER

Another way to relate a scary story is by having one person read a really frightening tale to the rest of the group, adding drama by using voices or sound effects in special ways. Be sure to check out Sinister Sounds on p. 59 for some ideas.

What You'll Need

- materials to make sound effects (see p. 59)
- a scary story or two (use the story on the following pages or pick out one from the *Scary Stories for Sleep-Overs* books)

Directions

1 Set the stage with special lights as suggested in Tell a Terror-Filled Tale on p. 72.

2 Have one person be the storyteller. Then choose someone else to make the scary sound effects. The storyteller and the person making the sound effects should have a chance to run through the stories at least once to practice.

3 Insert scary sound effects as suggested in the next story. Or you may want to choose your own sound effects and story.

TANTALIZING TIP

The key to telling a terrifying tale is to create mystery by using your voice. Practice lowering your voice or whispering to build suspense. When someone is being chased or is about to be caught, add excitement by using a voice that is quicker in tempo or somewhat out of breath. Figure out where long pauses would enhance the suspense. Most important, have fun!

74

THE COFFIN STOPPED

"So the girl is running through the haunted house, with this big old coffin chasing after her," Doug said, barely able to contain himself. He loved to tell jokes, and this was one of his favorites. The new kid in his class was the only person who hadn't heard it before.

"Yeah?" said the kid, looking a little confused.

"Then finally she's cornered, and the coffin is gettin' closer. [Scary Sound Effect: Drag heavy book slowly across hard floor.] It's looming over her, and just about to crush her. So what do you think she does?"

The kid was wide-eyed. "What?" he asked.

Doug paused for effect. "She took a cough drop, and the coffin stopped." Doug started laughing hysterically. "Get it?"

The new kid smiled weakly. "Yeah, I get it. Like, the *coughing* stopped. Cute, real cute."

"Cute? It's great!" Doug exclaimed. [Scary Sound Effect: Laugh hard, then start coughing.] "Ah, you're no fun," he said, walking away from the new kid. "You wouldn't know a good joke if it walked up and bit you."

Doug was certainly "bitten" by the joke. In fact, he couldn't get it off his mind. He thought of it everywhere, including during a funeral he had to attend with his family a week later. It was just awful, standing there, trying to be solemn, when this great joke was running through his head. It was even worse when he actually started chuckling as the pallbearers carried the coffin past him.

Then suddenly he felt just horrible. The daughter of the man who had died was staring at him. The look on her face gave him the creeps, and he tried with all his might to wipe the stupid grin off his face. He made up his mind to go up to her after the funeral and apologize.

"You were laughing at my dead dad," she said, walking up to him first.

"I . . . I wasn't," Doug stammered.

"Yes, you were," the little girl said. "And you're gonna be sorry."

By that afternoon, Doug had forgotten about the whole incident. In fact, he nearly forgot about the joke, too . . . until that night.

Waking up feeling cold and scared, Doug looked at the doorway to his room. Standing there was the very same coffin from the funeral! Doug froze in terror, watching the huge wooden box rock from side to side as it came toward him. **[Scary Sound Effect: Drag heavy book slowly across hard floor.]** He tried to scream, but no sound came out. Then the lid swung open **[Scary Sound Effect: Imitate the squeaking sound of rusty hinges.]**, revealing the dead man inside, and Doug howled in fear.

Suddenly he knew what he had to do. His hand darted to the drawer in his nightstand, and he quickly pulled out a box of cough drops. He shook a drop into his hand, and as the coffin was just about to crush him, Doug slipped the cough drop into his mouth.

And the coffin stopped.

Doug had to smile—he'd actually stopped the thing. "Hah!" he snorted defiantly, but as he did he accidentally swallowed the cough drop. **[Scary Sound Effect: Loud gulp!]**

Instantly the coffin started moving toward him again. **[Scary Sound Effect: Drag heavy book slowly across hard floor.]** Doug reached for the box of cough drops, but in his haste he dropped it and the drops scattered across the floor . . . out of reach! **[Scary Sound Effect: Drop many marbles or other small objects on a hard surface.]** Panicked, Doug dove for the box and shook out the only cough drop that hadn't fallen out. He quickly popped it into his mouth, and once again, the coffin stopped. Now looming over him, it was the dead man inside who was smiling. After all, how long could one cough drop last?

SPOOK SOUP

Serve up some scares by inviting your friends over to play this spine-tingling Name That Ghost Part game.

What You'll Need

- several items for body parts: pearl onions (eerie eyes); peeled baby carrots (frightening fingers); candy corn (terrible teeth); cooked spaghetti (gooey brains); gelatin (flubbery fat); thin, wet rope (horrible veins); raw hot dogs (icky intestines); small stones (killer kidney stones); damp sea sponge (broken brain)
- paper and pencil
- several bowls or pots, as large as possible

Directions

1 Gather the "body parts" of a dead ghost and put each part into its own bowl or pot. Use the list above for starters, or use your imagination to come up with some ghoulish ideas of your own.

2 Gather your friends and tell them that in the bowls or pots are the remains of a ghost. Each person must reach into the bowls or pots and try to identify the body part without looking. Give each person one point for each correct guess.

3 After everyone has felt inside the containers and received a score, announce the winner. Then empty out the bowls or pots and let everyone see what they were really touching!

77

THE FRIGHT IS JUST BEGINNING . . .

You now have all the tools you need to treat yourself—and some brave friends— to a frighteningly fun scary story sleep-over. And if you use your imagination, the possibilities are endless.

For lots more scary story fun, check out one of these collections of terrifying tales to read at your next all-nighter:

- **Scary Stories for Sleep-Overs**
- **More Scary Stories for Sleep-Overs**
- **Still More Scary Stories for Sleep-Overs**
- **Even More Scary Stories for Sleep-Overs**
- **Super Scary Stories for Sleep-Overs**
- **More Super Scary Stories for Sleep-Overs**
- **Mega Scary Stories for Sleep-Overs**
- **Scary Mysteries for Sleep-Overs**
- **More Scary Mysteries for Sleep-Overs**
- **Still More Scary Mysteries for Sleep-Overs**
- **Even More Scary Mysteries for Sleep-Overs**